Meet the
LATKES

Alan Silberberg

VIKING

Meet the Latke family. They're just like you and me.
Except they're potato pancakes!

That's Lucy Latke and her dog, Applesauce.

Mama and Papa are busy in the kitchen making fried jelly doughnuts.

Lucy's older brother, Lex, is reading comic books. "Get out of my room!" he shouts. Lex is a teenager. He doesn't care about anything.

I DON'T CARE!

But Lex *should* care. Because . . .

"Tonight's the night!" Lucy sings.
"It's the first night of Hanukkah!"

Oh, right. There's someone else in the Latke family.

"Tonight's not **HA**-nukkah," Grandpa says. "It's **CHHA**-nukah!"

"That's what I said." Lucy is confused. "Hanukkah."

Grandpa grumbles. "Say it with me:

"Thanks, Applesauce," says Lucy.

"Hmph," says Grandpa.

Getting ready for Hanukkah—

—the Latke family cooks and sings,

and decorates the house.

Except for Lex.
He still doesn't care about anything.

Then, after the menorah is lit . . .

And the dreidels are spun . . .

And the gelt gets gobbled . . .

. . . Grandpa plops Lucy onto his lap.

"Do you want to hear about the miracle of Chanukah, my little latke?"

"I do," Lucy says, biting into her last chocolate coin.

Grandpa begins with just a whisper. "First, you need to know about the BEES."

"Bees?" Lucy asks.

Grandpa nods. "Chanukah is a celebration of how the Jewish temple was saved from destruction. We celebrate this holiday thanks to the **brave bees** who buzzed and stung and fought to keep our people safe!"

I'm pretty sure there aren't any bees in the history of Hanukkah OR Chanukah.

"Feh!" says Grandpa. "Whose story is this?"

Lucy's eyes widen. "Were the bees big, Grandpa?"

"Big? They were huge! Giant!
They were **MEGA-BEES!**"

You mean
MACCA-bees.

"Nope," Grandpa says. "Definitely mega-bees.
And the biggest, bravest bee of them
all was . . . **JUDAH MEGA-BEE!**"

But Lucy can see it now: Judah and his swarm of giant bees, BUZZING and STINGING and FIGHTING to save the Jewish temple and the lives of everyone who worshipped there.

"And who do you think Judah and his big bees were battling?" Grandpa asks.

That's EASY. It was...

"ALIEN POTATOES FROM PLANET CHHHHH!" Grandpa booms.

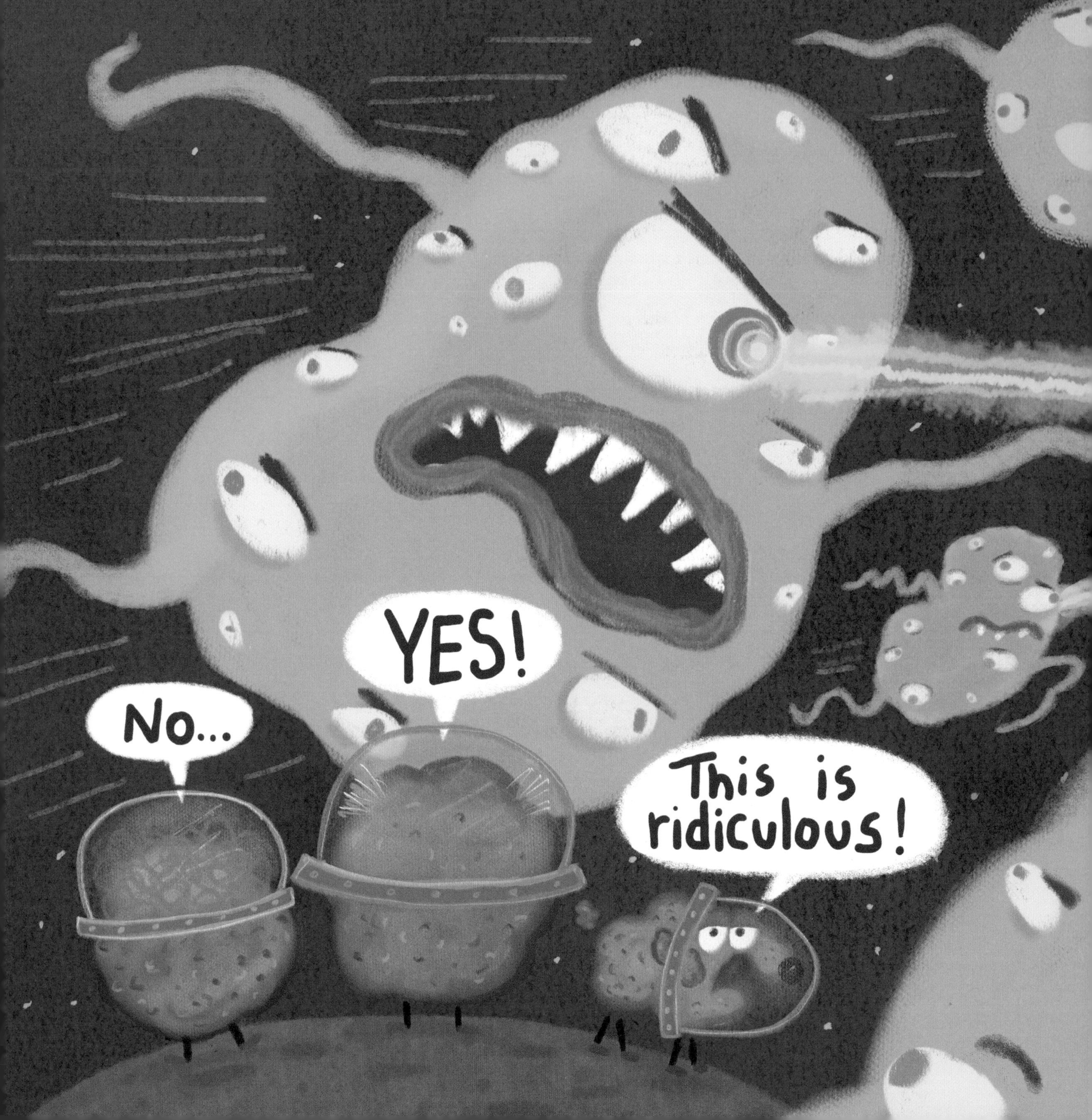

"Antiochus demanded that everyone believe in the same religion as he did," Applesauce goes on. "So for the Jews, that meant no more studying Torah, no more celebrating Shabbat, and never again worshipping God. King Antiochus and his followers almost completely destroyed the Jewish temple."

"The Mega-Bees plotted and schemed," Grandpa says. "And the next morning, when the sun rose on the temple, an enormous wooden dreidel stood in the village square. 'What could it be?' the alien potatoes all wondered. 'And why does it buzz?'"

Lucy waves her arms.
"I know! The Mega-Bees were
hiding inside the dreidel!"

"Smart latke!" cries Grandpa. "**Plitz! Platz! Plotz!** The Mega-Bees burst from the dreidel and **sliced** and **whipped** and **mashed** those tater tyrants into tatters."

WHIP!

"Tattered tater tyrants?" Lucy asks.

"Try saying *that* three times fast!" Grandpa says.

"And then . . . miracle of miracles," Grandpa says. "Judah Mega-Bee stood in the middle of all those spoiled spuds. 'What a waste,' he said. And so that great warrior added some EGG and ONION and a pinch of FLOUR to make something good from the bad . . . **POTATO LATKES!**"

Lucy's eyes and mouth are open wide. "So the miracle of Chanukah is that a long time ago Mega-Bees turned alien potatoes into latkes?!"

"Is that really true?"

Lucy points to her family's glowing menorah. "Eight candle holders. Eight days of the Chanukah miracle! And the shammes, the tallest candle to light all the others."

"You know what?" says Grandpa. "I like the dog's miracle better."

"Me too," says Mama.

"Me too," says Papa.

"I don't care," says Lex, stuffing his face with chocolate gelt.

HUG!

"Lex! You left your room!" cries Mama. "It's another Hanukkah miracle!"

Grandpa pats Applesauce. "Now that we all know the Chanukah story . . ." He gives a wooden dreidel a little spin.

"Who wants to hear about Passover?"

The Story of Chanukah (or Hanukkah!)

A long time ago, a tyrannical king named Antiochus tried to destroy the Jewish religion and everyone who believed in it. A group of Jews known as the Maccabees fought back and won. They took back their temple from Antiochus's army. But when they went to rededicate the temple's lamp, they found that they had only a tiny amount of oil left, not enough to keep the lamp lit for more than one day. The miracle of Chanukah was that this tiny amount of oil lasted for eight days, which is why some refer to the holiday as the Festival of Lights.

Antiochus: Syrian ruler from 175 to 164 BCE. He waged battle against the Jewish people and tried to outlaw all Judaic laws and customs. Antiochus's army destroyed Jewish temples and brutally forced Jews to worship pagan idols and gods.

Dreidel: A four-sided spinning top used in a traditional Chanukah game. Each side has a different Hebrew letter that signals a different outcome.

Gelt: Yiddish word for money. During Chanukah, gelt usually refers to chocolate coins.

Israel: The biblical Holy Land.

Latke: A potato pancake fried in oil, typically enjoyed on Chanukah with applesauce and sour cream.

Maccabees: The Jews who fought back against Antiochus.

Menorah: Candelabra with eight candleholders, one to represent each night of Chanukah, plus a ninth candleholder for the shammes, which is the extra candle used to light the others.

Passover: A springtime holiday that commemorates the Jews' liberation from slavery in ancient Egypt.

Shabbat: The Jewish holy day that begins every Friday at sundown.

Sufganiyot: Another Chanukah delicacy, these are round jelly doughnuts that are deep-fried and covered in powdered sugar.

Temple: A holy building where Jews go to pray.

Torah: The Jewish holy scroll, also known as the five books of Moses.

For Penelope and Grace and Clementine, and all
the little (and not so little) latkes everywhere!

VIKING
Penguin Young Readers
An imprint of Penguin Random House LLC
375 Hudson Street
New York, New York 10014

First published in the United States of America by Viking, an imprint of Penguin Random House LLC, 2018

LIBRARY OF CONGRESS CATALOGING-IN-PUBLICATION DATA IS AVAILABLE
ISBN 9780451479129

Printed in China

10 9 8 7 6 5 4 3 2 1